SAMSON & DOMINGO

By Gume Laurel III

An imprint of Enslow Publishing
WEST **44** BOOKS™

Please visit our website, www.west44books.com.
For a free color catalog of all our high-quality books,
call toll free 1-800-398-2504.

Cataloging-in-Publication Data
Names: Laurel, Gume.
Title: Samson & Domingo / Gume Laurel III.
Description: New York : West 44, 2024. | Series: West 44 YA verse
Identifiers: ISBN 9781978597099 (pbk.) | ISBN 9781978597082 (library bound) | ISBN 9781978597105 (ebook)
Subjects: LCSH: Gay teenagers--Juvenile fiction. | Dating (Social customs)--Juvenile fiction. | Identity (Psychology)--Juvenile fiction. | High school students--Juvenile fiction. | Sexual minorities--Juvenile fiction. | Football stories.
Classification: LCC PZ7.1.L387 Sa 2024 | DDC [F]--dc23

First Edition

Published in 2024 by
Enslow Publishing LLC
2544 Clinton Street
Buffalo, New York 14224

Copyright © 2024 Enslow Publishing LLC

Editor: Caitie McAneney
Designer: Leslie Taylor

Photo Credits: Cover AI Image composite/Shutterstock.com; Series Art (music/hearts doodles) blue67design/Shutterstock.com; (football/music art) Netkoff/Shutterstock.com, (text bubbles) itya_M/Shutterstock.com.

All rights reserved. No part of this book may be reproduced in any form without permission in writing from the publisher, except by a reviewer.

Printed in the United States of America

CPSIA compliance information: Batch #CW24W44: For further information contact Enslow Publishing LLC at 1-800-398-2504.

Find us on

For every band kid marching to the beat of their own heart.

Glossary
(in order of appearance)

chicharras: Cicadas
caliche: Gravelly, loose dirt
elote: Street corn/ corn on a stick
mijito: Son
tlacuache: Opossum
¡Fuera!: Go away!
¡Este vato!: This guy!
Apá: Dad
Ay, que lindo: Aw, how adorable
machismo: Macho
Amá: Mom
pan dulce: Mexican sweetbread
¡Válgame!: Oh, come on now!
concha: A shell-shaped Mexican sweetbread
¡Hijuesu!: Oh my goodness!
¿Quieres comer?: Want anything to eat?
¿A dónde?: To where?
curandera: A healer/ witch
Ven: Come
Ayúdame: Help me
Córrele: Run/hurry
raspas: Mexican snow cones

Samson's Hair

is too pretty for a jock's head.

Equal parts dark cocoa and milky smooth.

Runs longer than any high school math class.

I have no clue how he fits it all into

his football helmet for Friday Night Lights.

Samson Montaña & Domingo Paloma

We are the definition of star-crossed lovers.

    Pop vs. Indie

   Meathead vs. Band geek

Attending rival high schools
in the same city

    widens the divide.

But, it doesn't keep us from
texting each other around the clock.

"¿Y que?"
I say. *So what?*

"He's my football team's archnemesis!"

"Weslaco South High's entire football team
against one eleventh-grade quarterback?"
I say.

"You know how good he is, Domingo.
He's the star player of Weslaco North
High's team.
They're nothing without him!
And you'll be considered a traitor to
Weslaco South High
if you don't stop spending time with him."

Samson's Bright Yellow Mustang

is parked on the curb outside of my house.

    Samson stands beside it.
    His linen button-down drapes over
    his firm frame.
    Like curtains in the breeze.
    Atop Samson's head: his crazy-long black hair.

    Wrapped in a messy bun.

    In his hands is a bunch of flowers.
    White stargazers & fresh eucalyptus.
    Wrapped in crinkly paper.

    Before he hands them to me,
    Samson gives me a kiss.
    It lasts for only a second. But

    feels like the length of time
    between the Big Bang and today.

    Samson's solid bronze arms
    wrap me in a hug.

I feel safe.

Driving Down the Highway

"Where we headed, Samson?"
I ask.

    "Always wanting to know everything."
    Samson's left hand grips the steering wheel.
    His right hand holds onto mine.

"I only want to know what you have planned."

I squeeze his hand twice &

    he squeezes mine twice, too.

    "Always so impatient."

I gasp. Pretending to be offended.

    He rolls his eyes because
    he knows I'm faking.

    Samson squeezes my hand twice &

I do the same.

15 Minutes Later

"Close your eyes for the rest of the way,
Domingo,"
Samson tells me.
"Don't open them until I tell you to.
No peeking.
I want it to be
a surprise."

My Eyes Stay Closed

Even after we exit his Mustang.

    Samson guides me forward.

Rocks and dirt grind against the
 bottom of my shoes.
Birds surround us with songs. Like mariachis.
Even louder are the *chicharras*.
They rattle with the locusts.
Tree branches tug against my shoulders and
pants as

    Samson guides me forward.

No matter how much I want to open them,

    my eyes stay closed.

After a Couple More Minutes

the ground becomes rockier. Like *caliche*.
I nearly trip twice.

    "Almost there."
    Samson pulls me downward.

I take a seat on the ground.

    From behind, his arms
    wrap around my body

&

I sink into him.

    "You can open your eyes now,
    Domingo."

We Are Seated

beside the Rio Grande.
Its waters move strongly. Smoothly.
Splitting the land,

    north   from   south.

The river flows from the west,
where the sunset has turned the sky orange.
Like marigolds.

& purple. Like lavender.

& blue. Like irises.

& pink. Like tulips.

All of the sky's colors reflect off of the river.
Like a mirror. It's impossible to tell where one
ends and the other begins.

As if here and there
could be one in the same.

Samson's Stubble Tickles My Ear

"I've always wanted to share this view
with someone special,"
says Samson.

"Where are we, exactly?"
I ask.

"A place only I know about,"
he says.
"A place that now belongs to us."

"Which highway exit
did you take to get us here?"
I ask.

"Always wanting to know
everything,"
says Samson.

I can't help but giggle.

Summer Vacation's End

"I wish this summer
could last forever.
I don't want it to end,"
I say.

> "Do you think things will change?
> When we go back to school
> in a couple of weeks?"
> Samson asks.

I take a deep breath.

Then, I allow more
of my weight to rest
against him and say,
"I don't want things to change."

> "Do you think they will, though?"
> he asks.

"Only if we allow it,"
I say.

Crescent Moon

We watch the sun sink beneath the horizon.
With it, all the magic of a Texas sunset.

One by one,

    the stars appear. The crescent moon glows.
    Like a light tower.

It's the exact same shape as the night we first met.
During a bonfire at
South Padre Island.
After hours of taking turns catching the
other staring
from opposite sides of the dancing flames.

*I had stepped away from the rowdy crowd
for a moment of peace.*

    Samson had followed me
    out to where the sand met the tide.
    Where it was only us two.

    He told me his name &

I said,
"I know."

With my finger,
I trace the outline of the crescent moon.

    Samson takes my hand & kisses it.

I rest my ear against his chest.
Listen to his heartbeat.
It whispers our names over & over.

Moments After

Samson scratches the back of his head.
His messy hair bun bobs up and down.

"Undo your hair."
I glide my fingertips
over his forearm.
Like feathers.

    "I . . . I can't."
    He stops scratching.

"Why not?"

    "It's a mess to deal with.
    Getting it back in place
    takes so much work."

"I'll help."

    "No, really.
    It's okay."

Some People Are Particular About

how they fold their towels.
Which pens they use to write with.
How much chili powder goes on their *elote*.

    Samson is particular about everything
    that has to do with his hair.

Driving Home

We listen to Regina Spektor.
I sing loudly for Samson.

    "You should stick to
    playing the French horn,"
    he says,
    sticking his tongue out.

I keep singing.

    We sing the rest of the song together.

I'm mostly in key.

    He's closer to Hawaii
    than he is to the correct notes.

Samson Drops Me Off

"Ay, que cute,"
Mom says, smelling the flowers
that Samson gave me.
"I have a vase you can put them in, mijito."

"Es un gentleman. Claro,"
Dad says, nodding his head.

"Then why didn't he come inside
so he can introduce himself to us?"
Pablo says, still on the couch.

"Samson doesn't need an introduction.
You already know all about him, Pablo."
I roll my eyes.

"Sí, next time.
Tell him to come in so we can meet him,"
says Dad.

Next Morning

The flowers Samson gave me
make my room smell lovely. Like daydreams.
They're so overpowering, they mask the smell
of whatever Mom might be cooking for breakfast.

I hold the shirt I wore last night.
Breathe into it. Deeply.

Samson's scent of coconut and sandalwood
still clings to its threads.

I consider never washing it again.

Pablo Is Watching Me from His Bed

"Bet it smells gross.
Like a runover tlacuache baking in the sun!"
laughs Pablo.

I grab my pillow.
Chuck it at him with all my strength.
He catches it with ease.

    "Can't catch a football,
    but you can catch a pillow?"
    I taunt him.

With all his strength,
Pablo throws my pillow back at me.
He leaps out of bed, spinning his pillow.
Like helicopter wings.

Before he lands a hit, I grab my pillow.

We begin bashing each other.
Like hammers and nails.

"You're a Weslaco South Wildcat!"
Pablo shouts.
"Dating a Weslaco North Panther
is forbidden!"

"We're rival high schools!
Not nations at war!"
I shout back.

"Same difference, Domingo!"

Pablo lands a hit to my gut.
Knocks the wind out of me.

I hold my hands up to signal surrender.

He throws his pillow at my head.
Then marches out of our bedroom.

Getting the last word is usually my specialty.
But I still haven't caught my breath.

Recapping Last Night's Date

to the French horn section of eight.
We huddle together. Like ducks.
Beside the practice marching field.

"That's so romantic of Samson to take you there,"
Christine says.
Christine has never had a boyfriend.

"I bet he takes a different boy there every weekend,"
Ysela says.
Ysela has had too many boyfriends.

Leslie sticks up for me.
"You're jealous because
Charlie never takes you anywhere."

Ysela throws us her middle finger.
Charlie pretends like he didn't hear anything.

Roberta lies on the grass.
"So, it's getting serious?"
Her head rests on Nicole's legs.

"As serious as it gets in high school, I guess,"
I shrug.

"How long until you mess this one up?"
Josue sticks his tongue out.

Band Rehearsal

"Don't hold back, horns!"
Band Director Robison shouts
over the booming marching band
while she conducts from her podium.

Two bars later, the big French horn part
comes up.

We blast! Like a pod of fearless orcas!

"Beautiful job, horns!"

A bass drum player comes in too early.
The song turns into a train wreck.

"Hits of the '80s"

is this year's half-time marching band
performance.

Two upbeat songs.
One love song.
A medley of dance songs for the finale.

The love song has a French horn solo.

Leslie is our
section leader.
First chair.
A senior.

So, the solo goes to her by default.

Home From Band Rehearsal

Samson

Sounds like you really want that solo.

You should challenge her for it!

Me

If there's an audition for it, then maybe.

Samson

I'm sure you'll win the part!

North vs. South Scrimmage

Every year
on the last Friday of summer vacation,

    Weslaco North Panthers

    and

    Weslaco South Wildcats

have a football scrimmage.

This year's game
is held at Weslaco North's stadium.

Go Wildcats!

"You should go sit on the Panther's side
of the stadium, Domingo!"
Ysela tosses popcorn at my head.
"¡Fuera! ¡Fuera!"

"Go Samson!"
I cheer when I spot jersey #07
on the Panther's side.

Samson Is a Bulldozer

He cradles the football. Like a baby.
He charges forward. Like a bull.
He crashes into Wildcat players
with ease.
One after another,

Samson
sends
them
flying!

The Panther side of the stadium
cheers louder and louder.

Samson races down the field.

40-yard line
30-yard line
20-yard line

One last Wildcat stands in his way.
Buckled down at the 10-yard line.

#23
Pablo.

This Is a Football Game

but it looks like a WWE tournament.

> Samson crashes into Pablo
> and flings Pablo
> over his shoulder.
> Into the air!

The whole stadium winces
at the sound of Pablo colliding
with the ground. Like a ceramic mug.

> Samson spikes the ball down
> in the end zone. His fans go wild!

I shouldn't join them, but I cheer.

This causes my schoolmates to
scowl and boo at me.

Samson Is Swarmed by His Teammates

I lose track of which helmet belongs to him.
They jump up and down. Like it's a concert.

Moments after, they scatter.
I see him once more.

    He's looking in my direction.

I figure we're so far apart
that it's impossible for him
to spot me in the crowd.

Then,

he raises a closed fist to his chest.
He beats his heart twice &
points directly at me.

My cheeks blush. Red as rose petals.
It's impossible to hide my smile.

In response,
I place my fist over my
heart & beat it twice, too.

Friends seated around me become a mixture of
whistles and *awws* and *boos*.

Samson jogs back up to his team.
There's a smile branded on his face.

Scrimmage Continues

"He demolished your brother,
not even sixty seconds ago," Charlie says,
shaking his open hand toward Pablo.

Pablo has coaches at both of his sides.
They're helping him off the field.

He's limping.

Either way, he's still alive.

Probably only needs to walk it off.

"Pablo's fine, y'all," I say.

The few classmates who respond to me
are not on my side about it.

Good thing my parents aren't here.
That would have been a horrible first impression.

For the rest of the scrimmage,
everyone can tell that Samson holds back.

While he does score
plenty more
touchdowns,
he doesn't act like a
runaway train in the process.

After the Game

Dozens of students hang out
in the stadium parking lot.

I lean against Leslie's gray minivan.
The one the French horn section rode to the
game in.

"Brave of him to come
to the visitor side of the parking lot,"
Josue whispers into my ear.
He points his chin behind me.

    Samson is walking toward us.

On Enemy Territory

Everyone grows quiet.
I push past them and approach Samson.

Our smiles outshine the moon overhead.

I want to give him the tightest
hug ever. Let him snap me in two
when he hugs me back.

But this is the first time
he's come around my friends.

So, I give him a quick hug.

No kiss on the cheek.

Samson Meets the French Horns

"No wonder they call you Man Bun,"
Ysela jokes.
"That has to weigh twice your body weight."

    "Keeps my neck strong,"
    says Samson, easily.

Christine blushes.
The others smirk.

"Y'all know Samson,"
I say.
"Samson, these are the French horns.
Literally. Like, the whole section."

    He looks from right to left.
    Gives them a smile and a wave.

"What're We Doing After This?"

Samson readjusts the duffel bag strap
hanging over his right shoulder.
When he does this, his bicep flexes
to the size of a bowling ball.

> He notices me noticing his arms &
> he blushes.
> "If you have nothing planned,
> wanna go get something to eat?"

The horns all become
more attentive than
teachers watching
students take tests.
None of them says a word.
Their shifting eyes say it all.

"We were actually heading to Whataburger,"
I break the silence.

> "Oh, cool."

There's a Pause

as if Samson is waiting for me to invite him.

    "The one around the corner?"
    he asks.

"The southside location,"
I crinkle my nose.

We both know a northsider isn't welcome
at the southside Whataburger.

    "Cool then,"
    says Samson.

"You should come,"
Ysela butts in.
The others agree.

    "I mean . . ."
    Samson smiles sheepishly.
    His eyes dart back and forth
    between me and the others.

I force a smile.
"You should come."

Whataburger

Our party splits into separate booths.

Christine, Leslie, Samson, and I sit together.

"Order number eighty-six,"
says a server approaching our booth with a
tray of food.

    "Thank you."
    Samson trades
    an orange tent card with our
    order number
    for the tray of food.

Christine makes a pouty face.
The romantic bar is so low for men,
that buying me an eight dollar fast-food combo
is a touchdown.

We Eat

Our conversation is all about
recent shows we've watched.

When the conversation slows down,
I bring up another show.
Any random show that comes to mind.
Anything to keep the conversation away from
the topic of

our relationship "label."

"Did y'all finish the last season, yet?
Worst finale ever!"

A gust of wind sweeps through Whataburger
when the double doors fling open.
Everyone turns to the entrance.
The Wildcat football team pours in.

Pablo is with them.

Fight or Flight

"I'm pretty full."
I set down my cheeseburger.
I've only eaten half of it.
"Can't force another bite."

Ysela peeks over her shoulder.
Bobs her eyebrows at me.

> Samson sees her do this.
> He pretends not to notice.
> Takes another bite of his
> double-meat cheeseburger.

I place my hand on Samson's kneecap
and squeeze it twice.

Pablo places his order.
Then, he searches for an available booth.
Before he finds one,

he spots Samson.

Samson and Pablo Meet

"Really, Domingo?" Pablo approaches our booth.

Samson swallows his bite.
Wipes his mouth with a napkin.

> "Good game, bro."
> Samson goes to shake Pablo's hand.
> "You played tough out there."

Pablo doesn't shake Samson's hand.
He doesn't even say a word.

"Don't be rude, Pablo," I groan.

> "Oh, you're Pablo!
> Good to finally meet you, bro!"
> Samson is sincere.

"¡Este vato!"
This guy!
Pablo pops his chin up.

"Pablo, don't start," I say.
"Go eat with your friends. Leave us alone."

Pablo's teammates gather behind him.
If this were happening a couple hundred years
ago, they'd be carrying pitchforks and torches.

Babe

"Let's get out of here, babe,"
I say.

This causes
several football players to mimic me.
Like whiney parrots.

Babe! Babe!

I slide out of the booth.

> Samson starts to pile
> our trash onto our food tray.

Christine stops him and says,
"Don't worry, friend. I'll take care of it."

> Samson slides out of the booth
> and stands beside me.

Pablo puffs out his chest.
As if he's a boxer at a weigh-in.

Pablo's Bark

Pablo's machismo behavior is silly to me.

He can't even sleep alone in our bedroom.
Not without a nightlight.
And the top of his head is beneath
Samson's chin.

"Let's go," I say.
My hand slips into Samson's.

"Better do as he says, Man Bun!"
Pablo taunts.
"Don't make him wait!"

Samson's Bite

As we near the exit,
the football players start mocking Samson's hair.

>Samson's grip tightens. His neck veins turn
>into mountains. His eyes burn. Like volcanoes.

"Don't listen to them, Samson,"
I tell him.
"They're just bitter over
losing three scrimmages in a row."

One last football player stands
in front of the exit.
I walk past him without a problem.

>When Samson walks past him,
>the football player bumps
>his shoulder against Samson's.

>Samson's body is firm as steel.
>He's completely unaffected.

Instead, the football player clutches
his own shoulder. He whimpers
in pain. It's as if he bumped himself
into a brick wall.

Samson Drives Me Home

"I'm sorry that happened."
Samson's hands grip the wheel.
Like he's pretending it's the neck
of a Wildcat football player.

"You didn't do anything wrong.
It was their fault,"
I say.

    Silence.

"Glad you showed up that last dude,"
I say.
"He's always such a jerk.
Spends more time in ISS than he does class."

    "I didn't mean to do that to him."
    Samson's eyes are fixed on the road.
    "I didn't mean to hurt him."

"He gets what he gets.
Besides, you didn't do anything.
He bumped into you and hurt himself."

First Time for Everything

"You know,"
Samson starts to say,
"back at Whataburger,
that was the first time ever
you called me *babe*."

"Guess it sorta slipped out on accident.
Won't let it happen again. Promise."
I stick my tongue out & grin.

    One of Samson's dimples caves in.
    His grip on the wheel loosens.
    His shoulders lower from his neck.

"I know it's getting late,"
I say.
"But, want to meet my parents?
When we get to my place?"

Outside the Front Door

    Samson sniffs his violet tank top
    for the tenth time and asks again,
    "You sure I don't stink?"

"Chill out,"
I giggle.
"You're fine."

    "Fine enough to
    meet your parents
    for the first time?"

"You're a local celebrity.
You could show up dressed like a
clown. And they'd still be obsessed with you."

    "Local celebrity?"

"And also because you're the
hottest,
sweetest,
most real-life-Disney-prince
that has ever existed."

    "Ever?"

Inside

Mom and Dad are in the living room.
They're watching the nightly local news.

"Too bad about the scrimmage, Pablo,"
Dad calls to us. We walk up from behind.

"It's me, Apá,"
I respond.
"And I brought someone
for y'all to meet."

They Adore Him

"Ay, que lindo," Mom says.
She blushes when

> Samson gives her a proper
> handshake, with a kiss on the cheek.
>
> Next, he gives Dad a firm handshake.
> It has a teaspoon of machismo
> to impress Dad with.

Dad shakes his head approvingly.

> Samson says,
> "It's very nice to meet you both."

"We keep telling him,
'Domingo, yah, bring that guy in here
so we can meet him already!'"
Mom pats my shoulder.
"Pero, you know how he is."

"Amá, yah, por favor,"
I say.

> "Glad it worked out this time."
> Samson is extra articulate
> when speaking to my parents.
> As if this is a casting call.

Like, They Really Adore Him

An hour passes by.
It feels like only a couple of minutes.

The four of us sit at the dinner table.
We sip on coffee. Nibble on pan dulce.

"Wow, that's something!"
Dad is enthralled with
Samson's recap of his homecoming game
last year.
"Edcouch-Elsa, that's a tough team!
You must've played extra hard to win that game."

    "12–42!"
    Samson lifts his balled-up fist.

"¡Válgame!"
Dad's eyebrows shoot up.
Like he's a cartoon character.

Homecoming Game

"Who do the Panthers play
for homecoming this year?"
Mom dips a piece of her *concha* into her mug.

    "Actually,"
    Samson says, hesitant at first.
    He looks at me.
    As if I should know the answer.

I shrug.

    "Panthers play Wildcats this year.
    It's the homecoming game for both teams.
    Held at Wildcat football stadium."

Things Were Going Good Until

"¡Hijuesu!"
Dad throws his arms up.
"Wonder whose wild idea that was!
To make the Wildcats' and Panthers'
homecomings be against each other!"

"Pablo isn't going to like that,"
I snicker.

"I'm not going to like what?"
a voice sounds from the living room.
The front door slams shut.

Party Crasher Twice in One Night

"Hola, mijo."
Mom gives Pablo
a kiss on the cheek.
She walks to the kitchen counter.
"¿Quieres comer?"

"What am I not going to like, Domingo?"
Pablo stands behind and over me.

Samson says nothing.
His wide eyes fixed on Pablo
could roar no louder.

"Pablo, not now,"
Dad says, waving his hand.
"We have company."

Pablo stares back at Samson.
"Sup, Man Bun?"

Mom Scolds Pablo for Saying That

"Está bien,"
Samson tells Mom.
"It's almost midnight.
I should be getting home."

"Does the bun
turn back into a pumpkin
after midnight?"
Pablo taunts.

"Pablo, yah!"
Dad smacks the dinner table
with an open hand.
The spoons in our empty mugs rattle.

Pablo mumbles beneath his breath
while he walks away.
Headed for our bedroom.

Out on the Lawn

"Hopefully that last part
doesn't make your parents
think poorly of me."
Samson sits in his Mustang
with the windows rolled down.

"Nah, they loved you,"
I tell him.
"They'd trade you for Pablo any day."

I laugh, but

    Samson doesn't. He folds his lips in.

I Rest My Forearm

on the top of his Mustang & lean in toward him.

I say,
"Babe, you were wonderful.
There's not a chance
in the world that they
don't approve of you."

    "Say it again, Domingo,"
    he says softly.

"How they adored you?"

    "Before that."

"How you couldn't have
made a better first impression?"

    He rolls his eyes.
    He leans his head
    out of the window.

"Babe?"

I snicker before leaning in & kissing him.

I can feel
    both our lips smiling.

Midweek

Samson

Miss you!

Me

Miss you too!

Samson

It's weird not getting to see you as often as I did during vacation.

Me

It's only for this first week of school. Starting next week, band practice is only on Monday nights.

Samson

Football practice will be Mondays and Wednesdays But I'm down to pick you up after I'm done.

Me

So long as you're showered off, I'm down too.

Friday Morning Pep Rally

The marching band fills the gym with rhythm.
The color guard and cheerleaders dance
to our song.
The football team pours out of the locker room.
The entire student body is vibing along.

Preps. Geeks. Goths. Jocks.
It doesn't matter who you are.
If you're a Wildcat, then you have plenty of
school spirit. You let loose during school
pep rallies!

One by one,
the senior football players
take a turn speaking from the microphone.

"We're gonna crush the Mercedes Tigers!"

Everyone cheers!

"We're gonna tear the stripes off of the Tigers!"

Everyone cheers!

"We're gonna declaw the Tigers!"

This one gets a mix of delayed clapping and disapproving *ooohhhs*.

"Go Wildcats!"

Everyone cheers!

Wildcats vs. Tigers

It's an even match.
Nobody scores until the last minute
of the second quarter.

Tigers up by three.

At half time, our marching band
stands at attention on the sidelines.
Meanwhile, the Tigers' marching band
performs on the field.

Their show is based on *Phantom of the Opera*.
Thanks to the overbearing trumpet section,
you can hardly tell.

After they're done, we march onto the field.
We perform only the first song of our show.
All the parents in the stadium know it.
They're singing along to "Don't You Want Me"
while we play.

3-7, Wildcats

The buzzer sounds off.
It's the end of the fourth quarter.

"That's a win for the Wildcats!"
the football announcer blares
over the intercom.

We play the school fight song.
The stadium turns into
a hurricane of celebration!

"W-I-L-D-C-A-T-S, GO CATS GO!"

Back Home

Pablo and two of his teammates eat pizza
in the living room. They're watching
Scary Movie 3.
Line by line, they recite the jokes.

"Amá," I say.
I find her washing dishes.
"I know it's late, but is it okay if I go out with
Samson?"

"¿A dónde?"
She points her chin at the microwave.
11:23 p.m..

I say,
"Just to drive around.
I haven't seen him since last weekend."

"Bueno, okay.
Be safe.
Come back by one o'clock.
Pero, only for tonight."

Fifth Quarter

    Samson aimlessly drives us around
    our small hometown.

I refuse to let go of his right hand.
Even though it strains my neck,
I lean over the center console
to rest my head on his shoulder.

    "Don't fall asleep,"
    Samson says.

"I'm not sleepy," I say,
though my eyes are shut.
"It's just that this is the calmest
I've felt since the last time I saw you."

We come to a stop at a red light.

    He kisses the top of my head.

I hold his hand tight.

    He squeezes my hand twice &

I squeeze his twice back.

10 Minutes till Curfew

    Samson parks us outside of
    my house.

"Coconut shampoo?"
I bury my nose behind his ear.

    Samson flinches. Leans away.

"Is everything okay . . . ?"
I ask.

Uncomfortable Apology

"I'm sorry.
It feels weird.
Whenever someone
touches my hair."
Samson says this quickly.

"Sorry,"
I say.

"No.
No,
don't apologize.
You didn't
do anything
wrong.
It's me.
Not you.
Promise."

"Why does it bother you?"

"It's nothing.
Really.
I'm weird,
I guess."

Five Minutes till Curfew

I gently lift the back of my hand
to his hair. Like his bun is a stray cat.

>His nostrils flare.
>His eyes become wide as frisbees.
>His broad shoulders shrink in
>toward his neck.

"Is it okay if I . . ."
I begin to ask, but
then decide to stop.

>He's frozen.

My hand relocates to his lips.
I outline them with my thumb.
Then cup his cheek.

>"I'm sorry for being weird, Domingo."

>He gives me a kiss.

"There's nothing to apologize for, Samson."

We kiss again & again
until it's time for me to go inside.

One O'Clock

The front door shuts behind me.

"Traitor,"
Pablo groans at me
from the living room.

"How's your teammate's shoulder, Pablo?"
I mock.

15 Minutes Later

Samson

Made it home

Wanted to say I'm sorry, again.

Didn't mean to be weird about my hair.

Flipping my laptop open,
it instantly connects to my
phone. The text messages
from Samson open in a
chat box.

I continue our text conversation from my laptop.

Me

No worries. It's not a thing.

Samson

You sure?

Me

Promise.

Samson

Thanks, babe!

I'll make it up to you.

Me

There's nothing to make up for.

But, like, what you thinking??

Samson

Be ready at noon tomorrow so you can find out.

Bring swim trunks. I'll take care of the rest.

South Padre Island

is less than an hour drive away from Weslaco.

We drive over the causeway that
connects the mainland to the island.
Bad Bunny at full volume.
Windows rolled down.

Humid, salty air strokes my sand dune cheeks.
Seagulls and pelicans glide beside us.
Boats sail in the distance. Thin white lines
in the blue gulf water trail behind them.

Not a cloud to be seen.

Setting Up Camp

Samson digs our colorful beach umbrella
into the sand. Firmly. Without the use of any
tools.

"You make it look so easy,"
I say.

    "I'm a pro when it comes to
    beach umbrellas,"
    he smirks.
    "Better keep me around."

"I'll take it into consideration,"
I smirk back.

I unfold our single, XXL beach towel.

    Samson quickly takes one end of it.

    Together, we lay it beneath the umbrella.

I set down our bags
on the foot of our towel.

    Samson drags over our ice chest
    to hold down the head of the towel.

    "Teamwork!"
    Samson raises both of his hands
    into the air
    for a double high five.

I bite my bottom lip. A grin slips out.
I slap my palms against his.
"You're such a dork."

Sunscreen

"Domingo, I think four layers
is plenty."

I rub more sunscreen
over his wide, beefy back.
"You can never be too safe, Samson."

"Okay, okay,"
he chuckles.
Turns around.
Motions his
pointer finger
in a circle.
"Your turn."

Into the Water

I fight to keep my balance.
The water is up to my belly button.

    Samson slaps the water.
    Splashes in my direction.

"No!"
I gasp.

    "Oh, c'mon!
    You're already wet!"
    Samson looks away.

I creep closer to him. I bend
my knees. Using the force of the
next wave, I pounce out of the water.
Onto his back.

    Samson laughs as I pull him down.
    His head stays above the waves.
    Beneath the water, he grips my wrists.
    Pulls me closer.

My first instinct is to wriggle away.
To try and knock him down.

I hold back.

Tiny grains of sand are nestled in
the stubble of Samson's chin.
Drops of salt water and sweat drip
down the corners of his forehead.
His hair bun sits tight as ever
on the back of his head.
Loose hairs tucked behind his ears
wisp in the wind.

As I stare at him,

    he remains quiet.

Nearly an entire minute goes by.
All we do is stare into each other.
Silent. Flowing with the current.

I finally ask,
"Something on your mind, Samson?"

"Always wanting to know everything,"
he whispers with a weak grin.

We stay quiet a little longer.

I become lost in the universe
that his hickory eyes hold.

Without warning,

    he pulls me against his chest &
    hugs me tightly.

I was expecting a kiss.
Yet, this hug feels more special
than any kiss we've ever shared.
As if it were a pinky promise
and a confession, combined.

He holds onto me.
For an unusually long time.

I consider asking him
if everything is okay.

Instead, I keep the words
in the back of my throat.

Maybe I don't always
need to know everything.

Samson lets me go.

We stand as firmly as the tide allows.

    Samson turns his body toward the gulf.
    He lifts his arms out at his sides.
    Takes a long, deep breath
    of the heavy gulf wind.

    Samson is mountainous.
    The definition of strong.

    Yet, he doesn't use his strength
    to fight the rolling tides.
    He allows his body to rock and sway
    with each incoming current.
    In contrast with the
    crackling waves,

    Samson suddenly seems
    so fragile.

It makes me wish I could
protect him from everything
he can't protect himself from.

The Tides

make me feel powerless.
Their back and forth.
Their merciless force.
You face them
while standing on shifting sands
that give you little to no chance
for keeping sure footing.
Everything about coming into contact
with the tides is threatening.
With every incoming wave,
we drift away a little more.
We're pulled deeper and deeper
into the tides.

This is how I have felt about Samson
ever since I met him.

And it terrifies me.

Stargazing in the Sand

Music plays from my phone.
It mixes with the crashing water.

I sit beside Samson's head.
Legs crossed.

> His body lies flat
> over the beach towel.

> He looks up at me
> with a weak smile.

Like earlier,

> we stare at each other.
> Silent.
> For a little too long.

"Is everything alright?"
I have to ask him.

> "Nothing could be better than
> every second I've spent
> with you, Domingo."

Samson Shimmies His Body Over

    & rests his head on my lap.

The weight of his hair
feels heavier than the weight of his skull.
My hands cup his cheeks. As if I'm holding
a cloud.
I massage the sides of his jaw. My fingers trickle
toward his ear.

    At no point do our eyes look any other
    direction than directly at one another.

Without intending to,
my hands drift over his sideburns,

into his hair.

I yank my hands away.
"Sorry!"

"Don't be."
His large hands reach for mine.

Samson lays my hands over his hair
&
gently presses them down.

"I want you to, Domingo."

Samson's Hair

I pet his hair.
Every thick handful. Every strand.
It's smooth as river stones. Soft as a whisper.
As sturdy as the rest of Samson's body.

I touch his hair bun cautiously.
Not wanting to disrupt it any more than
a day on the island already has.

"You have to be using high-quality products
to keep your hair this healthy,"
I say.

    "Some three-in-one,"
    he tells me.

"Of course,"
I sigh.

Samson Sits Up

"I trust you, Domingo.
More than anyone I've ever
trusted before.
I've never felt as safe as I do
when I'm with you."

"I feel the same way, Sams—"

I try to say.

He cuts me off.

"No. I'm not telling you
so that you'll say it back.
I only want you to know
how deeply I feel for you."

It takes every ounce of my strength
to stay quiet.

I squeeze his hands twice.

The song we're listening to
comes to an end.

"Time After Time"

comes up next on my playlist.

    "Isn't that the French horn solo
    for your marching band show?"
    Samson asks.

I nod a yes while
softly singing along.

    He lays his head back on my lap.

We watch the stars overhead.

We've Done This Before

"Do you believe in past lives?"
Samson asks me.

"I never think about that sort of thing."
I answer.

"I don't either."

"Then why ask?"

"This moment feels like
we've done this before.
Me lying here.
Your hands in my hair."

"You're too much of
a hopeless romantic."

Samson softly sings along
as the song comes to an end.

His eyes are closed.
He can't see that

I'm smiling.

After Auditions for the Big Solo

Samson

No way! It was rigged! You should have gotten the solo!

Me

Well, I didn't.

Samson

Babe, I'm so sorry!

Me

It's cool. Really. Besides, it's her senior year. She deserves it.

Samson

Be outside your house in 10 minutes.

Me

Babe. I'm tired. And I haven't had dinner yet.

Promise. I'll be fine.

Samson

OMW. I'll be there in 10 minutes.

Samson to the Rescue

"You know what else?" I say.
"Leslie cracked the high note."
I whine to Samson.
My mouth is full of Whataburger.

    Samson & I
    are eating in his parked Mustang.

I go on.
"She only got the solo
because she's a senior!"

Samson says nothing.
He holds out an open packet
of spicy ketchup.

I dip the edge
of my cheeseburger into it.
Take another bite.

"Seniors shouldn't be guaranteed solos
just for being seniors.
And they should be able
to get through auditions
without cracking high notes!"

All Samson does is
nod his head & offer more
spicy ketchup.

Back in Samson's Secret Spot

Our sky becomes a mixture of orange.
Like tangerines.

& purple. Like plums.

& blue. Like berries.

& pink. Like dragon fruits.

>We watch the passing
>of another day.

>Samson wraps one arm
>around me &

I rest my head on his shoulder.

Where it belongs.

Sunset Blurs Daylight into Twilight

"You excited for homecoming
next month?"
Samson asks me.

"Sorta,"
I answer.
"It'll be the first time
we perform our full marching show.
From beginning to end."

He says,
"I'll be there, too.
I'll finally get to
watch you perform!"

My stomach fills

with butterflies.

We Stay Still

as the sun vanishes from view.
Nighttime spreads across the sky.
Like rainwater seeping into earth.

Twinkling stars begin to reflect off
the slowly moving river.
Like floating lanterns, reflected in the waves.

Everything is so calm. Peaceful.

    Until Samson asks me,
    "Can we talk?"

"Of course,"
I answer.
"Why? What's up?"

    "I have a secret,"
    Samson says.
    "A secret nobody has ever known."

My thoughts scatter a thousand directions at once.

I knew Samson was too good to be true.

I should have never trusted him.

"It's nothing bad,"
he says.

His definition of nothing bad
might not be the same as mine.

"Domingo, look at me."

My eyes stay fixed on the ground.

"Whatever you're thinking,
it's not that,"
he says.

I finally say,
"Then what is it, Samson?"

Samson Is Slow to Explain

"It's no secret that I'm strong,"
says Samson.

"No duh, Samson.
You're basically the Hulk!"

"Domingo, chill. Please."

I take a long sigh.
Zip-tie my lips shut.
Look up at him.

His eyes are swelling.
Like rivers after lots of rain.

"I'm stronger than any teenager should be,"
he says.
"Stronger than any human
should be."

Samson looks down at his lap.
Falling tears thud against his jeans.
He folds his strong arms over
his stomach.

"Samson,"
I lay my hand
over his forearm.
"What's going on?"

"It's so hard.
I'm scared to
tell you."

I Open My Mouth to Say Something

Several times.
Each time I do, I close it.
Not a single word comes out.

    More hot tears fall from
    Samson's eyes.

They boil against my arm.

    He snorts in his snot.
    Wipes his face.

    He finally looks back at me.

"Sorry.
I didn't
mean to
get like
this."

"You trust me. Right, Samson?"
I ask.

    "Yeah. Of course,"
    he says.

"Then you can trust that
I won't judge you.
No matter what you tell me."

    "It's not so simple, Domingo."

"You can tell me, Samson."

    "Okay . . ."

Samson's Secret

"So,
I'm really strong."
Samson starts.
 "Freakishly strong."

"Steroids?"

"No.
Nothing like that."

He pauses.

Samson says,

"I was born four months early.
Tiny. Weak. Sick.
All the doctors said I wouldn't live long.
My parents begged a curandera to do something.
Anything. Whatever it took to keep me alive.
So the curandera put her hand on my head and
enchanted me with a spell, saying,
'What grows from him will give him
greatest strength.'
Soon after, hair began to sprout from my head.
As it grew, so did the rest of me.
My bones, muscles, lungs, and heart.
I became healthy. Strong.
A complete miracle."

"My hair gives me
supernatural strength,"
Samson says.
"If I cut it off, I'll lose
all my strength."

"Samson—"
I try to say, but

    he stops me.
    He knows I need proof.

    Samson grabs a rock,
    winds his arm back,
    and throws the rock
    toward the sky.

It soars.
Above the clouds.
Keeps going and going.
Like gravity doesn't exist.
I lose track of it. But then it
becomes a flash of light before
leaving Earth's atmosphere. Now it's
a space rock headed for another galaxy.

My Jaw Is on the Ground

"Why keep a gift like that
a secret?!" I shout.

    "I'm not good at math.
    Language arts.
    Science.
    None of that.
    Sports is all I have going for me,"
    Samson tells me.
    "Sports are my only chance
    at getting into college.
    I have to keep the source of my strength a
    secret.
    If someone wanted to knock me down to
    size,
    all they'd have to do is
    cut off my hair."

"If it's such a big secret,
why tell me, Samson?"

"You're the first person to ever
make me feel this safe, Domingo."

"Samson, I couldn't defend you
against an angry chihuahua."

Samson says,
"I feel safe with you because
I can let my walls down around you.
I don't have to fake being tough.
Or fake being anything I'm not.
I may have supernatural strength,
but I get to be as vulnerable as I truly am
when I'm around you.
Because I trust you."

My Palms Brush Samson's Cheeks

& wipe away his tears.

I hold his bun of hair & kiss the top of it.

My arms wrap around his neck &
        his arms wrap around my back.

"Your secret is safe with me, Samson."

In the Frozen Pizza Section of H-E-B

"Tonight basically makes us
an old married couple.
You know that, right?"
Samson's shoulder keeps
the glass door propped open.

I look over the pizza selections.

"Next weekend is the homecoming bonfire,"
I tell him.
"The weekend after that is the
homecoming game.
I'd like to have a chill weekend
before we end up super busy
with all that."

I Pick Out a Supreme Pizza

With his finger, Samson draws
a goofy-looking smiley face
in the fog of the inside of
the glass door.

"A modern-day Picasso,"
Samson puffs out his chest.

"With a lopsided nose like that?"
I giggle.
"Yup. I'd say it's Picasso inspired."

He grabs me from behind.
Squeezes & tickles me.

We laugh the whole way down the aisle,
headed for the checkout area.

Checkout Lane Four

"Just the pizza?"
The cashier smacks
spearmint gum like a cow.

I turn away. Look at the
candies beside his register.

I can tell the cashier is staring at me.

    "Yes,"
    Samson reads the cashier's nametag.
    "Thanks, Rolando."

    Samson rubs my back.

Rolando nods,
"Ohhh. I see."

    "Okay?"
    Samson pays with his debit card.

"This your type now, Domingo?"
says Rolando.

Worst Case Scenario

    Samson waits for
    me to respond.

"You gonna introduce
me to Man Bun, Domingo?"
says Rolando.

"Let's go, babe,"
I tell Samson.

"*Babe?* Ha!"
Rolando mocks.
"Still a simp.
Aren't you, Domingo?"

    "What's your problem, man?"
    Samson's ears boil red.

Rolando Holds Out Samson's Receipt

"Y'all have a fun night."
Rolando won't shut up.
"Condoms are in aisle number two
if you need any."

    Samson swats Rolando's hand.
    Faster than the meteor
    that barbequed the dinosaurs.

    He grabs Rolando
    by the collar of his uniform.
    Lifts him high into the air.

    "I don't know who you are.
    I don't care to hear it from you,"
    growls Samson.
    "You're going to apologize
    to my boyfriend."

Rolando's Face

becomes a tomato.

    Samson's grip tightens.
    He shakes Rolando.

"Suh . . . suh . . . sorry,"
Rolando tries to speak.
His face changes
from a strawberry to a beet.

I wish Samson
would throw him
across the grocery store.

He could if he wanted to.

    Samson tosses Rolando
    into checkout lane number five.

Driving Away

Neither of us says a word in the Mustang.

    Samson drives us to his house.
    Both of his hands
    grip the steering wheel.

    "He deserved worse,"
    Samson finally speaks.

"He's probably the worst person I know,"
I respond.

    "How could you be friends
    with a guy like that, Domingo?"

"I'm not."

    "Well, then how do you know him?"

"Rolando is . . ."
I try to say.

    Samson says,
      " . . . Rolando is . . .?"

I finally say,
"Rolando is my toxic ex."

Samson Parks Us in His Driveway

"I can't picture you with that guy,"
says Samson.
"You're a sunflower.
That dude is sewer sludge."

"I'm not a sunflower, Samson."

"Yeah, you are."

"I'm not.
I maybe once was a sunflower.
Before Rolando."
I take a long breath.
"After my relationship with him,
I became a rose."

Samson says,
"A rose is also a flower."

I say,
"A rose has thorns.
A rose knows how
to stay guarded. To
keep people at bay."

Coming Clean

"I busted Rolando lying to me, Samson.
So many times. And I forgave him.
Each of those times.
Rolando said I was too needy. Too emotional.
He eventually ghosted me, and that was that.
And it sucks because I didn't do anything
to deserve all that.
I was thoughtful. And caring.
And patient.
And he wasn't."

My chest feels like cement.

I say,
"What I got out of that relationship is
the fear of falling for someone else.
And then going through it all over again."

My bottom lip trembles.
It makes my voice shaky when I say,
"I always want to know everything
because I used to be with someone
who kept me in the dark about everything.
I need to know all the answers
because all I had with my ex was questions.

"Why didn't he care?
Was I not good enough to be cared for?"

"It's not that I still have feelings for him.
Trust. Not even a little bit,"
I continue telling Samson.
"It's just . . . that sort of hurt is a grease stain.
It clings.
Holds on.
No matter how hard you scrub.
Makes you feel dingy. Used. Ruined."

Samson holds my hand & says,
"You're not ruined, Domingo.
You're fragile.
We all are.
Even a supernaturally strong freak like me.
Our fragility is what makes us human."

My head leans onto his shoulder.

My thoughts slow down.
For the first time in years.

After a Long Pause

"Back at H-E-B,
you called me your boyfriend,"
I tell Samson.

    "Well, yeah,"
    Samson says.
    "You're not dating some other guy.
    Are you?"

"No. Only the one."
I chuckle.

    Samson rolls his eyes.

"Really, though.
You consider me your boyfriend?"

    Samson says,
    "Well, yeah.
    I care about you.
    You care about me.
    We're only dating each other.
    Is that not the definition of
    being boyfriends?"

Boyfriends

"I guess I never saw it that way. Because you never asked me to be your boyfriend," I tell Samson.

    "Is that how it works?"
    he asks.

"Well, according to
Article Seven, Section B of
The Official Gay Teen's Guide to Dating—"

Mid-Sarcastic Response

Samson interrupts me.
"Do you want to be my boyfriend, Domingo?
Officially?"

I cup his cheek &
then run my hand across his hair.

"With all I am, Samson.
The way you've trusted me with your secret,
I will trust you with my heart."

A Typical Afternoon

Me
> Hey, Hercules!

Samson
> You know I hate it when you mention my super-strength.

Me
> You know how many people would kill for your gift?

My phone signal dips.
So I jump on my laptop.
Continue our conversation there.

Samson

I wish I could control my strength.

Me

What if you cut your hair shorter? Maybe that'll lessen your strength.

Samson

Unless my hair is completely shaved off, I stay supernaturally strong.

Me

Have you tried shaving it all off?

Samson

As much as I hate this gift, the idea of not having it scares me. I don't know how weak I'd become without it.

I think that's why I refuse to ever cut it. The reminder that I could be made weak is nerve-racking.

Mom Interrupts Our Conversation

"Domingo! ¡Ven!"
she calls.

"Hold on, Amá!"
I shout.

"¡Ayúdame, Domingo! ¡Córrele!"

Mom And I Are Home Alone

She's balled up on top of the kitchen counter.

"There, Domingo! There!"

A roach.

They don't scare me.

I trap it with a disposable cup.
Then, I slide a newspaper flier beneath the cup.
This seals the roach inside.

"Domingo! Squash it!"

I rush out the back door.

Into the backyard.
Reaching the wooden fence,
I toss the roach free, into the alley.

Reentering My Bedroom

Pablo has my laptop.

Opened.

On his lap.

I Scream Louder

than my mom did about the roach.

"Get away from my laptop, Pablo!"

I dive toward him.
Swipe the laptop from his hands.

"I was only checking my email, Domingo!
To see if I had homework or not.
Why you freaking out?"

"You have your own laptop for that, Pablo!"
I shout.

"Mine takes forever to turn on!"
he complains.

I Scan My Laptop

Nothing is open. Except for
Pablo's email account.

"What did you see on here, Pablo?"

"Nothing, Domingo!
Why are you freaking out so badly?"

"Were my chat boxes open?"
I don't believe him.

"What shady business you hiding, bro?"
He tries to turn things around.

"Pablo, answer me!
Were my chat boxes open?"

Pablo shouts,
"I didn't see anything, Domingo!
Stop freaking out!"

"Pablo . . ."

He begins to walk out of our bedroom.

"I swear, Domingo.
Ever since you started
hanging around Man Bun,
you've become even more annoying."

Raspas

Samson & I
buy *raspas* at the city park.

I order a grape "Wildcat Fury."

    He orders a cherry "Panther Blood."

My lips are dyed violet &

    Samson's are dyed red.

    "Looks like you have lipstick on.
    It's kinda cute."

"Just kinda?"

Our lips are now maroon.

"Excited for tomorrow's game?"
I ask.

    "Mostly so I get to hear you play that solo,"
    says Samson.

Samson eats another scoop of his *raspa*.
Then he says,
"I'm still not convinced that
you had nothing to do with
Leslie getting sick enough
to sit out homecoming."

I say,
"If I had supernatural powers
that could cause appendicitis,
you'd be first to know."

Our lips are now maroon-er.

"So, I have a
surprise gift for you, Domingo."

"I have a
surprise gift for you, too, Samson."

Homecoming Garters

Samson & I uphold the Texas tradition of gifting a garter to your boyfriend for homecoming.

> His—
> Purple, silver, white.
> Clanking cowbells. Sequins.
> Puff-paint footballs on the ribbons.
> A white mum with a #07
> at its center.
>
> &
>
> A single black bow
> with glittery treble clefs.

> Mine—
> Purple, silver, black.
> Clanking cowbells. Sequins.
> Puff-paint music notes on the ribbons.
> A black sunflower with a French horn at its center.
>
> &
>
> A single white bow
> with glittery footballs.

Thursday Night

Pablo turns over in bed.
That's now six times in ten minutes.

"Take a melatonin already,"
I groan.
"Homecoming is tomorrow.
We both need to sleep."

Pablo says nothing.

"Is something bothering you or what, Pablo?"

    "Go dream about Man Bun, Domingo."

"His name is Samson!"

Pablo Stays Quiet

"Why are you such a jerk about him?
You don't even know him, Pablo."

> "You've only known him for a few months.
> You don't really know him, either."

"He's a nice guy,"
I say.

> "You said that about Rolando,"
> Pablo says.

"What does Rolando have to do with anything?"
I ask.

> "It's the same as with him.
> You get excited. Get attached.
> Defend him. Then cry over him."

"Samson is nothing like that!"

> "We'll see, Domingo. We'll see."

"Samson is the definition of a perfect boyfriend!
He's compassionate
and considerate
and actually cares about my happiness."

Pablo groans,
"Ay, Domingo."

"Samson makes me feel like I deserve
healthy love.
I wish you could be happy for me,"
I tell Pablo.

"I don't want you to get hurt, Domingo."

"I won't."

"You could though.
I want to protect you from that.
Everything that could ever hurt you.
You're my baby brother and it's my job
to keep you safe."

"That's not how growing up works."

"I want it to, though.
I don't want you having to cry over guys who
didn't deserve you.
I don't want you feeling
unworthy of love."

"Placing my heart in another man's hands
doesn't mean it's guaranteed to break, Pablo."

"It's more likely to break
in another man's hands
than it is staying hidden
inside your chest, Domingo."

"When it comes to Samson, I like my odds."

"You really trust him,
don't you?" says Pablo.

"I wouldn't be up late arguing
with you about him if I didn't."

"Do you love Samson?"

"I don't know yet.
Like you said,
it's only been a few months."

We both huff out once
in place of laughter.

"He's a good guy, Pablo.
I wish you'd give him a chance."

Homecoming

Cheerleaders shout and excite the fans.
Marching bands play loudly from the stands.
Color guards raise, twirl, and spin their flags.
Footballers huddle and clap their hands.

Homecoming!

Homecoming!

Go Teams Go!

Let's Play Ball!

Just 15 seconds into the game,

                         Samson scores a touchdown.
          Same as he did during the scrimmage game.

                              He spikes the ball.
             Beats his heart twice & points to me.

I'm sitting with the marching band.
Nobody around me cheers for Samson's score.

Instead,

they whoop and holler for me when

I beat my heart twice & point back at him.

Second Quarter Ends

12 to 54.

Panthers in the lead.

Halftime

The drum major shouts,
"Wildcats, at attention!"

"Attention!"
The marching band shouts back.

We freeze in place.

Feet—together.

Shoulders—back.

Heads—up.

Hearts—with pride.

Onto the Field

The drum major counts down,
"Four! Three! Two! One!"

The drum line plays a cadence.
The band marches onto the field.

Everyone on the home side of the stadium
stands up.

They clap and cheer! As loudly as they do for
the football players and cheerleaders!

The marching band comes to a stop.
We are all in our starting positions across
the field.

Seconds till Showtime

The marching band stands still.
We are waiting for the drum major
to count us in and start the show.

The crowds continue to cheer.
There's thousands of them.
My nerves sizzle. Like sparklers.

The drum major climbs up her small tower
on the 50-yard line.
That's where she will conduct the
marching band.

The stadium grows quiet.

The drum major raises her arms and
counts down,
"Four! Three! Two! One!"

Songs One and Two

Every step is exact!
Every note is in tune!
Every move is perfectly timed!

Everyone in the stadium eats it up.
Like tamales on Christmas Eve.

Once Song Three Begins

I break out of formation to
stand beside the drum major's tower.

My garter jingles as I shiver.
Nervous from all the faces staring at me.
I stare back at them. Every single one.
Searching for Samson in the sea of people.

"You got this, Domingo!"
a voice calls out from the crowd.

My Eyes Turn

to where the voice comes from.
It's Mom. She's sitting beside Dad.
I look to their left. Expecting to see Samson.

All I find is an empty seat.

Samson is nowhere to be found.

It Wasn't Supposed to Happen Like This

I want to stop the band.
Stop the half-time countdown on the scoreboard.
Hush everyone quiet.
So I can find where Samson is hiding.

My favorite person.
The only one I want
to hear me play.

Sadly,

I can't stop time.
Not even for myself.

Everything feels wrong.
There's no time to feel right.

The moment comes.
I raise my mouthpiece to my lips.

As I play my solo, parents sing along.

About stolen secrets deep inside.
About drums beating out of time.

Autopilot

Not one note is missed.
No space is too wide or too slim.
A flawless performance the rest of the
way through.

I can't remember any of it happening.

The Show Is Over

The marching band gathers beneath the
bleachers. Drinking Gatorade. Eating popcorn
and pickles.

Not me.

I return to my seat.
Remove my hat.
Lay my French horn down beside me.

And

do all I can to hold back my tears.

End of Halftime

Both football teams jog out of the locker rooms.
They rush onto the football field.

Panther #07 is nowhere to be found.

Then, one of the Panther coaches
exits the locker room. With Samson.
He pats Samson's helmet.
Pushes Samson in the direction
of his team on the field.

    Samson is running a little lopsided.

Third Quarter

A player tosses the ball to Samson.

> Samson doesn't rush forward.
> Like he always has before.

There's shouting between players.

> Samson finally moves forward. But after three steps, he's tackled down.
>
> To the ground.

My Jaw Drops

Everyone in the stadium gasps.
I have no clue how there's any air left to breathe.

A referee blows his whistle. The Wildcats
reposition themselves.

The Panthers circle Samson.

              He's still on the ground.

People Shout from the Stands

"Walk it off!"

A teammate holds his hand out to Samson.
He pulls Samson up.

The football gets tossed again.
This time, to a different player.

A Wildcat sprints toward Samson.

>   Samson gets knocked back.
>   Like a lifeless doll.
>   He falls onto the ground so hard
>   that his helmet flies off.

Every Panther and Wildcat
gasps at the sight.

>   Samson's hair is gone.
>   It's completely shaved off.

Stunned

"Since when?!"
Christine rushes up to me.

I try to answer. But any response
stays hidden from my tongue.

>   A coach from the Panther's side
>   runs up to Samson.
>   Stands him up.
>   Carries him
>   to the sidelines.

I rush down the bleachers.
Push my way out of the stadium.
Zigzag through the parking lot.
Reenter the stadium through the visitor's side.

I approach a chain-link fence.
The one that separates the bleachers from
the field.

Several feet ahead on a bench

    sits a slouching #07.

"Babe!"
I shout.
"Behind you!"

Samson looks over his shoulder.
He sees me pounding my fists
against the chain-link fence.

When he approaches me,

he removes

his helmet.

He drops it to the ground.

Through the Chain-link Fence

our fingers intertwine.

"Samson, what happened?"

   "They knew, Domingo."

"Who? How?"
I ask.

   "Did you tell them?"
   Samson whimpers.

"Samson . . . I . . ."

Samson begins to sob.
He presses his forehead against
the fence.
There's fresh cuts all over his head.
Not one strand of hair has been spared.

Through the fence,
I kiss his head & then press my forehead
against his.

We cry together.
Like overwhelmed toddlers
who can't talk yet. Who can't
tell you exactly where it hurts most.

There's Yelling on the Field

"Back off!"
Wildcat player #23 yells. It's Pablo.
He pushes one of his own teammates.
"Back up off me!"

"Stop that!"
a referee slides between them.

"What's good, bro?!"
Pablo's teammate pushes past the referee.
"You're all talk, Pablo!"

Football Field Brawl

Pablo grabs his helmet by the face mask.
Lifts it off his head.
He has a fresh maroon bruise under his
right eye.

"Wait . . .
Did Pablo do this to you, Samson?"
I ask.

    "No, Domingo.
    Pablo was the only one
    who defended me."

Pablo dodges his teammate's swinging fist.
He lunges forward.
Knocks his teammate to the ground.
The entire Wildcat team rushes in.

Panther football players try to help.
Wildcat football players think they're
under attack.

The field becomes a gladiator ring!

Coaches blow whistles.

Announcers call for peace.

Nothing works!

Homecoming is cut short. Nobody wins.

Samson's coaches
grab his shoulders
and pull him away.

I shake the chain-link fence.
Cry for him to come back to me.

   He doesn't.

Instead of Sleeping That Night

I text him.
Over and over.

Me

u okay?

please call me.

just tried calling you.

unsure if you saw.

call me.

please.

i miss you.

u there?

are we okay?

When the Sun Rises

I check my phone for the millionth time.
Still no response from Samson.

My lungs are cold. Like I've been breathing
in ice. My chest feels like the moon is pressing
down on me. Keeps me stuck in bed. Forces my
heart to beat faster than it should. I grip the
mattress, because I swear that the room is
spinning, while all the world has come to a stop.

I had finally found someone who got me.

All of me. Even without having to explain the complicated parts. The parts I've kept hidden from everyone else. And I got him. Including all the parts of him he kept hidden, too. We fit together, like lock and key. Opened the door to a hopeful tomorrow.

Now, he's gone.

The door is locked.

I have nobody to call home.

Early Evening

On the front porch,
I keep doing what I've done all day.
I read over old text messages from Samson.
Pics. Memes. Links we've sent each other.
Wait for those three bubbles to pop up,
so I know he's about to text me.

They never pop up.

Not once.

Churning Gravel

calls from the curbside.

My favorite yellow Mustang.

> Samson is hard to recognize
> without his hair.
> Even harder,
> with a frown.

I try to smile at him. But can't.

This feels like a breakup.

My Face Loses Color

"Hey,"
I say.

"Hi,"
says Samson.

I've been dying to see Samson all day.
Not like this, though.
Fresh scabs on his head.
Dried-tear crust around my eyes.

Holding my breath because this is likely the end.

Behind me, the front door opens.

    Samson nods in that direction.

Pablo approaches.

The skin around his eye is dark violet.

    Samson fist-bumps Pablo.

Pablo's Confession

"Thanks for coming, man."
says Pablo.

    Samson nods back to Pablo.

"I lied about not seeing
your conversation when
I had your laptop, Domingo,"
says Pablo.
"I read about Samson's hair.
I told my teammates.
We planned to ambush him before the game.
After me and you talked Thursday night,
I realized what I did was wrong.
I stopped my teammates from
cutting his hair before the game.
But then they did it during halftime."

    "Pablo tried defending me,"
    says Samson.
    "That's how he got that shiner."

Pablo says,
"I'm sorry. To both y'all."

"I didn't mean to ignore you, Domingo,"
says Samson.
"I'm sorry that I did.
I needed space.
I needed time.
Will you come for a ride with me?"

"Pablo, how could you?!"
I yell, prepared to give him
a second black eye.
"Babe,"
Samson reaches out. Takes my hand.
"He apologized.
That's all he can do at this point."
Pablo says,
"For what it's worth,
our team's out for the season
for jumping Samson. And for
that whole battle dome thing."
"Pablo—"
I want to cuss him out,
but Samson stops me when he says,
"Pablo's the reason
I'm here right now, Domingo."

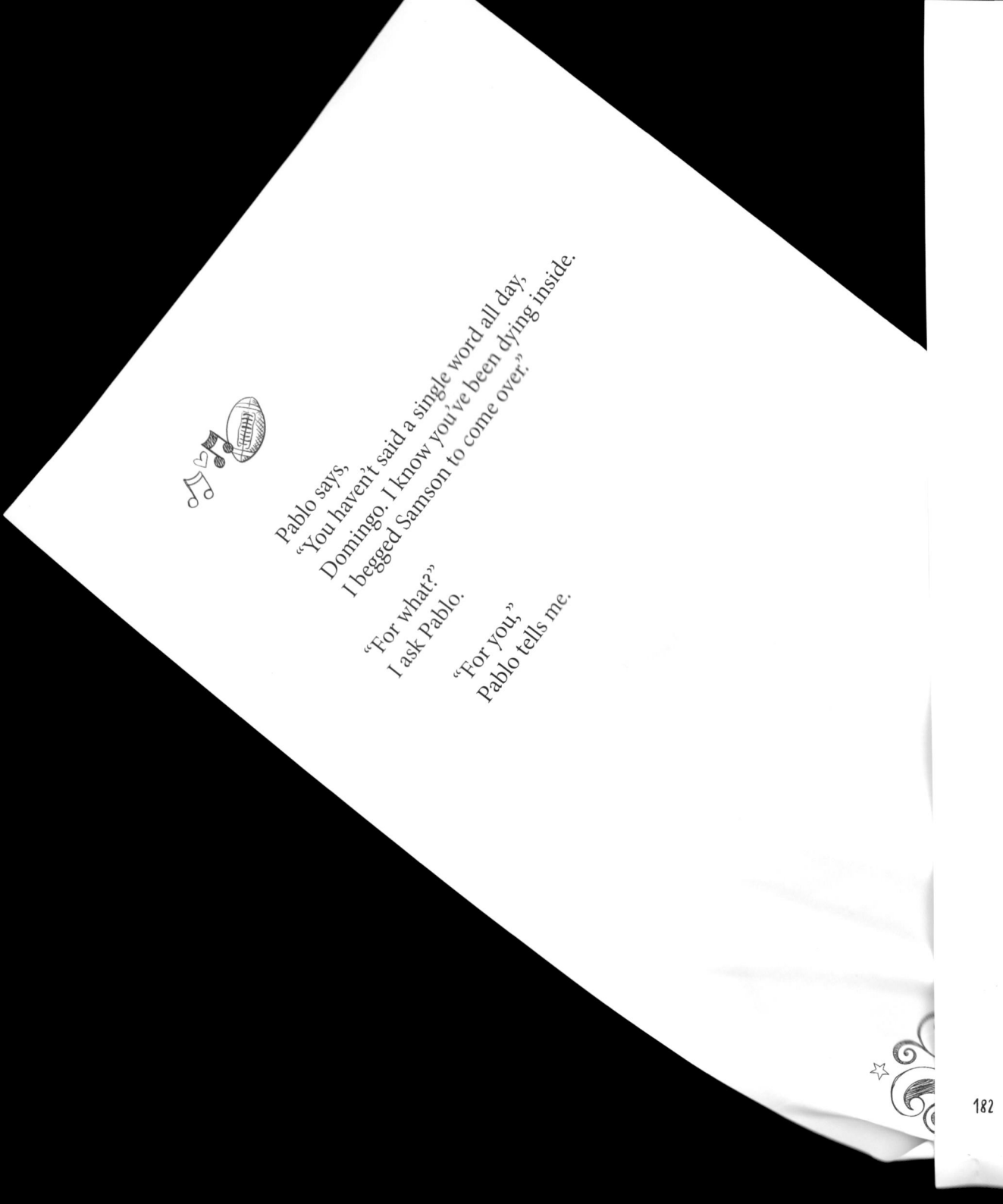

Pablo says,
"You haven't said a single word all day,
Domingo. I know you've been dying inside.
I begged Samson to come over."

"For what?"
I ask Pablo.

"For you,"
Pablo tells me.

Samson & I Drive Down the Highway

Out into the country.

Leaves are changing. From green to
gold & bronze.

It's late afternoon. The sun is low.
The air is cooler than it was the first time
he brought me out here.

"Why did you think
you'd lose me, Samson?"
I ask.

    Samson says,
    "Because I was scared that
    you wouldn't like me anymore.
    If I didn't have all my strength."

I say,
"I didn't fall in love with your strength, Samson.
I fell in love with your fragility."

"In love, Domingo?"
he asks.

"Yes. In love, Samson,"
I whisper.

Our Crescent Moon Becomes Visible

The evening sky glows orange.
Like sunstone.

& purple. Like amethyst.

& blue. Like sapphire.

& pink. Like rose quartz.

As it always has,
maybe always will,
the river runs beside us.

> Our reflection in the river
> constantly changes
> as the waters flow onward.

I See the River Differently Than Before

It does nothing to divide us.

Instead, the river
connects us.
Binds us.
Pairing our strengths & fragilities.
Turning two independent bodies of earth

        into one.

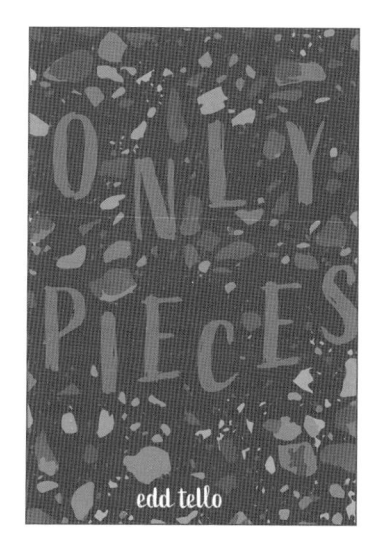

CHECK OUT MORE BOOKS AT:
www.west44books.com

An imprint of Enslow Publishing
WEST **44** BOOKS™

About the Author

Gume is a Texan, native to the Rio Grande Valley on the southernmost border. For the past decade, he has dedicated himself to crafting literary works that promote inclusion and showcase diverse characters with intersectional identities. The bulk of Gume's writings are focused on underrepresented groups, especially those from the communities he is a part of: Latine and queer. When he isn't writing, Gume can be found getting lost on a hiking trail with his dogs Blu and Mouse. For more info on what he's up to, check out GumeLaurel.com and @TX.Author.